Sweet Caroline´s

For Daisy and Sunny,
my Great Danes, my heart.

Chapter 1

I love critters. I believe that most people who aren't neurotypical connect with animals in an extraordinary way. Animals fascinate me. It's more than the unconditional love and the je ne sais quoi of fur or feathers or anything different than my own sensitive skin-that douceur of an animal's fur, that indescribable comfort… the soul piercing eyes of a dog or a wild animal who's surrendered trust to a rescuer during times of peril. I think it's because I've never met an animal that was an asshole just to be an asshole. It's been my experience that animals only want to be understood, even if they just want you to understand they want and need to be left the fuck alone. Isn't that what we all want? To be understood? Even animals that act out and choose violence. Don't they always have a natural reason? Even if it's one we can't understand? Is that our shortcoming? I want to think my cat, Turkey, is an asshole for ambushing me at my desk and biting me in the fucking face this morning, I understand he's frustrated because he wants to go outside. It's obvious because he sits at the window and his meows clearly darken from mewling pitifully to angry yowls that make me think he's going to shorten my lifespan. I feel super guilty because I know he doesn't understand why I won't let him outside with my dogs. That should either the hawk or owl I've seen and heard spot him; his ass is theirs. Judging from Daisy's and Sunny's success in catching anything, I don't think the Great Danes would help even if they wanted. I've learned that if I have specific bursts of playtime with the cat before the dogs go out, I can mitigate some of that feline rage. I wish I had Seth's magic touch. He's a legitimate critter whisperer. Our neighbors used to have a pet rabbit who used to escape and come to find my husband when he was in the yard. A rabbit. Like how? What? Your dog got out? Come see if it's found the way here? All the other lost dogs have. It's wild to me. He can literally lay hands on any pissed off animal and they melt like they had an appointment for a free massage. It's one of the many things I love about him. He didn't grow up with animals. He wanted to. His mother would never have allowed it. During our first year together, I found a sleeve of photo prints he'd taken of puppies he'd found trapped in a garbage sack by the curb. His mother had found the stray litter and hoped they'd make it onto the garbage truck circulating for the day. They don't have a relationship. My experience growing up was different. Growing up on a small farm, I experienced everything that goes with a rural East Texas farm from gathering eggs and ringing the necks of chickens and butchering a cow to squirrel and deer hunting. Just like Seth, I've felt the trauma of animals. One of earliest memories of my cousins was everyone standing around a large pile of newly skinned squirrels. The skinned bodies gave little spasms, nerves firing blindly beneath the exposed flesh, as if the memory of movement hadn't drained out yet. I'm pretty sure I felt sick for weeks afterwards whenever momma started dinner. Don't get me wrong. I'm not vegan. I wish. Having grown up only knowing fried vegetables, I struggle to appreciate the lifestyle. Even now we enjoy a great steak on rare occasions. For the most part I happily live my life grazing on various trail mix flavors supported by some super processed microwave meal. I do not eat chicken off the bone. Any food w th bones bothers me. When I was in 7th grade my parents sent me to an outdoor survival sleepaway camp. They didn't see it that way. It was packaged as a back-to-nature Christian camp in the deep woods – lots of praying and singing hymns around a lake type escape to make kids appreciate the Lord's work. That was my first year as an overnighter. One week into the two-week camp we took a three-day excursion on foot into the deep woods of East Texas. Our meager supplies included rations like peanut butter and crackers and water pulled directly from a spring fed stream. While I don't know how far we traveled, we'd gone through incredibly dense woods and slept under the stars for two nights. Mid-morning on the third day we emerged from the deep woods, filthy, exhausted, in pain (two of us had gotten stung by scorpions during the night), and hungry. So hungry. We were told we'd finally get a hot meal. The last hot meal we had was on the morning we left. We gathered around the central campfire for directions and the first and only time I've ever had paper bag bacon and eggs. That last morning as we gathered wood to make a fire, I thought about that breakfast. Rolling the top of the paper bag to make a reinforced cuff and inserting a stick under the cuff to make an extension pole to go over the fire. Trying to hold the bag low enough to get some crisp on the bacon without starting a pork Hindenburg. Cracking that egg over the hot greasy bag and wondering if it would all crash through to the dirt. That taste. It felt like I'd never had bacon and eggs before. That's the hot food I thought we were getting. Imagine my surprise when a beat-up old Ford pickup loaded to the max with caged chickens pulled up to where we were gathered. I soon learned that this was part of the experience. We were to kill, gut, pluck, and prepare the chickens right there. Seventh graders. The mean girls from my church yowled like they were on the menu. At the time I prided myself on being a tomboy. I found most girls were mean to me, but I fit in with the boys. Maybe it was because I grew up with two older brothers, maybe it's because the guys were nice and I got enough verbal abuse at home. Plus, the boys at church camp were a lot nicer than the girls and I had a crush on one of the boys from McKinney. So, I did what any girl does who desperately wants to fit in and impress the boy she likes, I went Annie Oakley – "I can do better." I carried wood and water like the boys and when every girl there declared she was too good to murder a chicken, I thought to dig deep into my roots as a farm girl and got to the task. I don't know the exact number, but it felt like I killed at least twenty chickens that day. My weak little kid hands taking several tries to break necks, effectively torturing the poor birds. After that was pulling the guts out, then I think we blanched the carcasses before plucking. When I yanked at the feathers, they came out with this awful, wet pop — like the skin didn't want to let them go — and the tiny holes left behind made me look away. They left behind a field of empty pores — raw little punctures staring up at me like a colony of tiny mouths. Something in me recoiled so hard it felt stitched into my nerves. I sometimes wonder if trypophobia doesn't come from ancient trauma at all, but from moments like this — some poor kid forced to pluck a bird long before they had the stomach for it, and their mind never healing around the holes. Even the sounds messed me up. When the carcass opened, the organs spilled out with a thick, sucking squish, the kind of sound that makes your teeth hurt. The guts clung together as they fell, connected by slick ropes of membrane that stretched before they snapped. And the bones—those tiny, hollow things cracked like brittle twigs, tendons snapping after them with a wet little flick. Even now, the memory of that sound sits in my throat. That's why I can't eat chicken on the bone. Every bite sounds like that.

Chapter 2

Whew! I had to stop and shower after that. That memory always makes me feel dirty. I also decided to freshen my hair. Both center me. Sometimes my mind feels like one of those Tibetan sound bowls with thoughts ringing WOOONG WOOONG WOOONG around in my head. Showering always softens the reverberations until I feel focused again. I think I get some of my best ideas in the shower. Dye-time showers are always a bit different, the color flowing across my body and circling the drain is the color I use to match my natural shade, vivid rusty looking cooper red – I often gaze at the drain and am reminded of similar memories with blood draining. Morbid I know, but it does look like blood. Although I spent my childhood being squeamish, I was grateful that I eventually found scientific curiosity. That coupled with an ingrained altruism won the day and made me everything I am today. I almost forgot to introduce myself! My name is Caroline. I've been a vet for the last twenty-three years. I'm sure you've seen one of my dog groomer's vans or doggie daycare minibuses around. I'm proud to say I've made Sweet Caroline's the gold standard for pet care. But you know that already, don't you? People

always want to know how I came up so fast —
how a nobody from nowhere could build a pet
empire damn near overnight. I was rumored to
start with one pitiful little shelf rented at one of
those hipster cafés where desperate middle-aged
somethings resale trinkets and baked goods to
carve out a meager existence. They write articles
whispering about my mysterious backers,
assuming I've got some shadowy corporation
propping me up. I never correct them. I let them
spin on their own stories. Obfuscation is a
kindness, sometimes. It keeps them out of the
parts of my life that don't belong to them. But the
truth? The real truth? I'm the biggest cliché you
can imagine: the money came from a lottery
ticket. Not a glamorous heiress. Not a business
prodigy. Just someone who survived on peanut
butter and crackers in the woods, someone who
plucked chickens and gutted squirrels and grew
up with more horror than help. People think my
rise is mysterious because they don't understand
what it looks like when a feral kid finally catches a
break. They think it must be corporate money, or
a trust fund, or some secret investor. No. It was a
ticket bought on a bad day. Winning was the easy
part. Finding trustworthy people -that was hard.
When the checks cleared, I had more than
enough to launch operations in over twenty states,
hundreds of grooming vans on the road, and a full
backend corporate network. People assumed a

big investor. They never knew the ticket numbers. Most of the money? This is most of the money. I dreamed about this place since I was ittle. Seth, my husband-you may not remember him, we designed it while still in vet school! He put my engagement ring on the rolled up completed plan! Isn't that the cutest thing ever? This whole compound is everything I'd ever dreamed of giving an animal, and then some. A magical place with no pain and nothing but love. A place that technically doesn't exist, but here we are.

I should tell you about the surgical wing! My surgical wing alone is enough to make seasoned veterinarians go quiet. A full bone-and-joint theater stretched the length of a barn, its walls paneled in brushed stainless steel that drink in the light. Mmmm. Every surface - seamless, built for sterility, built for precision. Custom hydraulic tables that can shift angles with a whisper. Arthroscopes and laser rigs … same specs used in elite human orthopedic centers. Imaging? I have it all. A full-body CT scanner built for animals up to 1,800 pounds. Two digital X-ray bays with ceiling-mounted track systems so smooth you could push them with a fingertip. Ultrasound suites that can pick up a kitten's heartbeat through a blanket. My fluoroscopy room looks more like NASA than a veterinary clinic…

Recovery is its own world. I hate to think an animal is ever in pain…or scared…So - Quiet dens lined with heated floors and cedar slats so animals wake up warm and unafraid. Our rehabilitation team? If you'd have told me years ago there was a human worth the effort I would've called you a liar but this team, our family…We have a hydrotherapy lane with programmable current, flanked by tempered-glass walls that turned opaque with a tap for privacy… Oxygen therapy pods sized for everything from a toy poodle to a mastiff. I hate to quote Jurassic Park's John Hammond, but "I spared no expense". If an animal needed it, I got it. If a surgeon could dream it, I built it. This is the best veterinary facility in the world.

You're gonna want to duck your head.

We started with facilities for the animals. I've got miles of fenced free-range pasture broken into sections for species, with shelter so pretty they could be in high-end architectural magazines: cantilevered barn roofs, insulated walls, temperature-controlled interiors, and soft bedding that gets replaced daily. Seth's team diverted a local stream for fresh water. Salt licks. Platforms for goats. Mud wallows for pigs. Ah, they are the cutest little fuckers! Do you like pigs? Heated winter pens – even cooling for heat alert days!

You might want to clench your ass because it's a little bumpy in through here. I've been telling Seth to fill those holes.

Staff Housing. That is where my pride lives. If you're turned around, we're just north of the rehab building. Yeah, so I couldn't do without my staff so each of these cabins for a better term, is absurdly comfortable and shockingly luxurious. Because these are not outsiders. They are my people. Staff, yes — workers, caretakers, veterinary techs, behaviorists — but also extended family and those few friends I trust more than I ever trusted my blood. We live together on the compound not just to tend to the animals, but to tend to each other. That was the promise: safety, belonging, and a purpose larger than ourselves.

Oh, this is cool.

We call this the common lodge. It's beautiful inside, massive cedar beams and a stone fireplace so massive you could practically step inside it. The furniture is so soft and deep, best thing ever when you're exhausted after a night of chaos. I've got bookshelves running from the floor to the beams, crammed with everything from veterinary journals to old paperback mysteries. There was always a pot of coffee on, and usually a pot of stew simmering nearby because someone is always hungry and someone is always cooking.

You can't see them from here, but the other side had these gorgeous windows that frame the pastures beyond, so when you're resting inside you can still see horses grazing, dogs playing, or one of our new goats.

We're not headed around there though. No. No. No. You know? It's the darndest thing, we never measured it. I don't guess it matters, does it? You see that fence running there to the right, sorry — you're left? Well Daniel and Mr. J were back in one of the little cluster of clearings in the woods, putting up that fence. Down yonder a bit it dips, according to J it was an accident, but I think they were horsing around, Daniel loses a tooth. Now you tell me how you manage to knock out a tooth putting up fence posts? However, it happened, not one of the other thirty people on the ranch heard what Seth and J called the shrill of a crack headed banshee. I was closest -up feeding the goats-I didn't hear a thing until they came flying over the horizon honking like madmen. Through the woods on the other there-that's just woods. Woods have a way of swallowing up a man's screams. Acoustic suppression and all.

Sorry, forgot to tell you to duck.

So anyway- You good back there?

Like I was saying, what you saw up front — the surgical suite, the recovery bays, the canine enrichment yards, the community lodge with the massive stone fireplace and all my people laughing in the evenings — that's what most folks think is the whole operation. That's the showpiece, the postcard, the part that gets grant money and good press and donors sending checks with little paw prints in the margins. That's where we live in harmony with all creatures.

It's real, too. Everything I told you is real. We are a family. We are thirty-three strong. We live here, work here, eat together, look out for one another. We've built something beautiful that outsiders can only dream of. This is paradise.

Now… we're heading into the thicker pines. Smell that? Gets swampy back here, like the air's turning solid. Woods don't mind holding secrets; that's why this section is perfect for what we do. Look to your right — no, wait, never mind, you can't. Habit. You'd see the tree line open if your face wasn't pressed into your own shoulder blades right now. We're getting close to the point of this all. Yes, I built a world class rescue. But seeing what monsters like you do with no conscious…that highlights the real need doesn't it? That's a point — a moral, natural, God-honest point — that some animals don't just need rescuing. Some need justice.

And here we are. Can you tell I've given this tour?

This here — this is what we like to call the Justice Barn. See, folks always think animal rescue is just lost animals or pets dumped at the pound. But they don't know half of what's out there. They don't see the burn scars, the broken bones, the chemical sores, the starvation, the bodies dumped like trash because some bastard didn't feel like paying for food. Or some poor soul like Buddy. You don't even see the sick irony in naming him that? Fucking psychopath! That dog will be deformed for the rest of his life because of you! He was weeks away from a torturous death-IF you'd have let him life that long! I'm going to make sure Buddy gets the love he deserves. I'm going to make sure Buddy gets the justice he deserves.

Chapter 3

There you go. I see your eyes opening. Good. We were wondering how long you'd stay under from the blow you took earlier. Not that it matters — you weren't getting anything for the pain regardless. You earned the clarity. Go on, try to breathe. Feels wrong, doesn't it? Like your own face isn't sure where it's supposed to sit anymore. Don't panic. That pulling you feel isn't the tape or restraints. That's you. Or I guess I should say: that's what you did to Buddy living on your own jaw. Blink if you hear me. There we go. Now listen close, because you're awake enough to understand every word. What we did here — what I did here — this was one of the hardest justice cases we've ever had. The Thirty-Three argued over this one for hours. Days. Everyone agreed you deserved justice; that wasn't the question. The question was how to deliver it in a way the universe would understand. In a way Buddy would understand. Some cases are easy. Someone shoots a cat for fun? We already know how to settle that. Balance is balance. Math is math. But what you did…the slow, steady torture…the way Buddy's face collapsed into itself...

That's a different kind of evil. That's commitment. That takes a level of neglect you have to rehearse. So we had to match it with intention. Deliberation. Not just a reaction. Now, about what you're feeling: Your mouth won't open the way it used to. Your jaw is set tight — tighter than it should ever be. Your lips don't quite meet in the middle. And that dragging ache along both sides of your face? That's the pressure memory. The tightening. The collapse. I didn't do it to you. I did it for you. So you could live inside the shape you forced onto another living creature. No sedation. No comfort. No mercy. If Buddy lived every waking second of his life in pain, then you can live the rest of yours in the truth of it. Try to speak if you want. Did I mention I also severed your vocal cords? You can try to whine, I guess. Appropriate, if you ask me. You're waking up to justice, plain and simple. And trust me… this was the gentle version of what half the committee wanted. Now that you're conscious, I'll walk you through the rest of what comes next. Not because you deserve the kindness — you don't — but because Buddy deserved someone narrating his pain, and nobody ever did. You can't see it yet, but when I tilt that mirror toward you…you'll understand. But first, let me tell you exactly what I did. See that tray over there? I didn't bother to wipe anything down. Didn't sterilize a thing. Didn't even rinse. Some of that dried brown smear you see on the clamps? That dog shit. I used that edge to clean my shoes. I didn't scrub, didn't wash, didn't even flick the dirt out from under my nails, and damned sure didn't wear gloves. You torture a dog? You don't get the courtesy of my hygiene. You notice the smell yet? It's sour, metallic, a little sweet at the edges. That's what happens when instruments sit too long with last week's work still clinging to them. I left it all there on purpose. Thought of it as... seasoning. Now, onto the part you're really wondering about: Your jaw used to hinge freely. There was space for breath, for chewing, for laughter — for whatever it is people like you do when they think they're safe in the world. But Buddy? Buddy didn't get that luxury. His face compressed slowly, hour by hour, day by day, and you cannot tell me you didn't see-at least the rotten leftovers you gave him kept him alive long enough for us to find him.

So what I did — in broad strokes, mind you — was recreate the effect. You felt pulling when you woke up, didn't you? That tight, burning tug running from the corners of your mouth back toward your ears like invisible wire? That's not swelling. That's your new structure. Your flesh is sitting where I made it sit. And believe me, it did not want to cooperate at first. Human tissue fights back when it's moved places it doesn't belong. It spasms. Twitches. Resists. You were twitching right along with it. Looked like a dying catfish. And the more you thrashed, the more it started to look like some kind of messed-up line dance gone wrong. So we put music on. Now don't look at me like that. We always play something to pass the time during justice cases anyway — it keeps folks calm, keeps the mood light, reminds us this is still work, not anger. And considering the way you were kicking and twisting and doing whatever that little seizure-shuffle was… well, somebody put on "Footloose." You should've seen it. A whole room full of us trying not to laugh while you convulsed like you were auditioning for the worst country wedding of all time. Even Seth started tapping his boot. Hell, I caught myself humming along. Now, I'll admit, with you flinging yourself around like that, some of my cuts ended up a little jagged. Not ideal, but not a problem either. I had to pull everything tight anyway — tighter than nature ever meant it to go — to get the artificial collapse right. The tension had to be uneven, had to drag, had to feel wrong, so honestly, you did half the work for me with all that thrashing. But don't you worry. The jaggedness is part of the effect. Part of the justice. Part of the message you'll be wearing for the rest of your life. You'll also notice that certain parts of your face feel raw. Exposed. Like the air is brushing places it shouldn't be able to touch. That's normal for what you are now. Skin doesn't like being rearranged. It's stubborn. It complains. It bleeds in its own time. Speaking of which, you bled like a stuck hog for a minute there. Messiest damn thing I've ever seen. Didn't bother to stop it either — figured it was cleansing. We just let it pool. The table's still tacky from where it dried. Yeah, I did call it "cleansing." Not in the spiritual sense — I don't care about your soul — but in the practical one. Even filthy blood washes things away. Dilutes things. Moves things around. And considering how many bacteria, spores, and God-knows-what else were clinging to those instruments, I figured the flood at least rinsed the worst of it off before everything settled back into your wounds. Think of it like sweeping a dirty porch with a hurricane. It doesn't make anything clean, but it rearranges the filth enough to buy you a little time. Not much time. Just a delay. A grace period before the inevitable. Because you are going to get an infection. There's no maybe here. We all talked about it — the Thirty-Three. And the real question wasn't whether infection would set in, but how. Sometimes it starts with heat — skin warming up until it feels like someone tucked a coal behind it. Sometimes it starts with swelling, slow at first, then sudden, like something underneath is pushing to get out. Sometimes it starts with color, too — that bruise-purple shade that creeps like a stain in water, like it knows where it wants to go. If you're lucky, it'll be the kind that turns everything numb before it turns everything black. If you're unlucky, it'll be the kind that keeps you painfully aware of every throb — every beat of your own heart hammering bacteria deeper into places they were never invited. Could be fever. Could be trembling. Could be hallucinations — the kind where the shadows breathe with you. And there's always that one nightmare version, the one where the infection doesn't stay politely in one place, oh no — it travels. That one makes a man feel like bugs are walking around under his skin, tapping their little feet against his nerves. Nature picks. But whatever it chooses…it won't choose gently. You tortured a dog. The universe has a sense of humor about these things.

Oh, don't try moving your mouth. You'll tear what little is holding it together. Buddy had to learn not to struggle too, and I think it's fair you get the same education. What you're wearing now isn't a wound — it's a sentence. And every time you try to smile, yawn, cry, or speak, your own face is going to remind you what you stole from that dog. Now breathe slow. The pain spikes if you rush it. We've got time. Hell, I've got all the time in the world. And speaking of time…Go on, turn your head just a little — yeah, like that. I want you to see something. That board on the wall over there? That's our Days Without Incident board. We use it in the justice wing only. Now, normally folks put something like that in a warehouse, you know, to brag about safety records. But we don't do safety out here. We track something different. You. Well, you and the ones before you. See, this is where I'm going to write your number every morning. Day 1. Day 2. Day 3. However long you've got. Every sunrise you're still breathing, I'll change that number. Every sunrise you're not… I'll reset it to zero and wait for the next bastard who earns a spot here. You want to know the highest number we've ever gotten up to?

Ninety-seven days. That was old Gerald Tinsley. Then we had Darla Porter — remember her in the news? Left her dogs in a car to get her nails done and tried to act shocked when they literally cooked to death in the Texas heat? She barely made it to three. Thought she could beg her way out of justice. Thought pretty women got exceptions. Not here. Not with us. Not with Thirty-Three pairs of eyes watching the scales. You're starting fresh. You're our new tally mark. And I want you to understand something real clear: This board isn't here for motivation. It's not here for progress. It's not even here for us. It's here for you. Every day you wake up in this room, you'll see that number. And every day it'll tell you the same thing: "You're still here. You still owe. And the only thing deciding when you're finished is the balance you tipped." There's no dignity here. No redemption arc. Just the slow tick of days being counted by people who stopped believing in mercy. See, folks like to pretend justice comes stamped with a seal, signed by a judge……and sometimes that's the only qualification justice requires. Tomorrow morning, you'll be Day 1. We'll see how far you make it.

Chapter 4

Day 1

Morning, sunshine.

Don't try to sit up. You made that mistake the first time, and I had to peel you off the mattress like wet paper. Just lie there and breathe... or whatever that noise you're making counts as. That right there — that deep, grunty, almost pig sound? That means everything's settling into place. Tightening. Inflaming. Arguing with itself. A body screams in its own language when it's hurting real bad. You hear that? Yours sounds like a hog. I mean that in a flattering way — it means you're healing exactly as expected.

I am glad to see your eyes are open, though. That's good. I want you awake for story time. I told you last night that you'd start Day 1 today. And look over there — on the wall, see? I already marked it. Now, the first ten days are my favorite. Fear and pain will make even the meanest son of bitch beg for their life before the resolution of justice becomes clear to them. We'll do our best to guide you. You will receive no meds, no comfort, no kindness except whatever scraps I toss your way. You lived through the night so you're a fighter – the cruelest ones always are. The universe wants her time to enlighten you.

Hey! Hey! You will stay awake when I'm speaking to you! Do you understand? Thank you. Now. This is how each day will go, if we remember and if we feel like it, someone will bring you food or water whenever we get around to it. After all, you are all the way back here. Anyway, when I come, I would like to tell you about your predecessors. We'll start with the longest-lasting one…mean ass old Gerald Tinsley. I like to tell his story on the first day because you have the strength to pay attention. Gerald Tinsley. Ninety-seven days. Still the record. Sorry. I said that. You know? You fucking stink already. I'll never get used to the smells…

Ok-So you probably remember the name, right? — made the news, even back then. Gerald lived out off of Lavendar Rd. in that trashy trailer park? He had a dog he didn't deserve which he half starved. He only made the news after he broke that dog's spine because it barked. What kind of an asshole hits a dog with a sledgehammer because it barks? Left it lying there in the dirt like a broken toy until the sun went down. I know the Sheriff wanted justice served. The whole fucking system is a joke. Punishments never fit crimes. Not unless a punishment is thoughtful and done with a higher purpose. That's what we do here.

So anyway-Gerald was the first-well everything. First for Seth. First for me. We'd been well established as a world class veterinary and animal rescue facility and respected for, geez, damned nearly a decade at that point. As I'm pretty sure I told you when we met, animals are the priority. I made sure we were fully functional before getting the new team to the core mission of justice for all the suffering you've caused. Sustainabi ity is vital. Why go to all this effort if we hadn't thought of – well, everything. Smart people you know?

You're gonna want to try and shield your eyes because this quick wash is going to sting like the devil. Can't let you out the easy way.

Smart people! I've been so fortunate to meet and surround myself with smart people! Good people. Every one of them would do anything for the cause – for poor souls like Buddy to get rescued and the justice they deserve. An operation of this scale doesn't just take a lot of money; it takes a lot of planning. Planning and finding those like-minded loving souls to support every aspect of each plan with passion.

Look at me yammerin' away! I won't tell you to stop squirming, but I will tell you that you're making it worse. Burns like hell, don't it?

There. You eat – that. Yes, it's what it looks like, an inadequate amount of the cheapest made kibble – mostly offal and gristle – and half a can of the nastiest canned food we could find. Bon appetite. You'll probably want to get on that sooner rather than later. Flies are bad back here. You'll see.

Anyway-Gerald wasn't much of an eater-he much preferred his whine. I think I'm funny. Trying to gurgle out "fuck you"? Good luck trying to articulate the "f" sound again – or any sound. You're drooling and you smell like dead ass already.

AS I WAS SAYING. To my understanding, Gerald got the dog from a drinking buddy who'd had a bad car wreck - DUI no doubt. Problem was that the dog barked. And barked. And barked. Evidently, that poor dog never stopped alerting due to the constant barrage from wildlife as his trailer was edged by thick woods and in line with the tasty garbage cans. Not that it bothered Gerald, he was usually too drunk to wake from the incessant barking. It became his problem when he got warned by property management. It only took one little memo and the police ended up getting called because he just had to catch that poor girl in the office and give her hell. I think he gave hell to everybody and probably the devil too.

We had always dreamed of really changing the world. When I saw the story on the news, I knew it was the perfect opportunity. You see, we are the professional consultants that regularly work with law enforcement and judicial offices in any and every case involving animal abuse or neglect. I did the necropsy in Gerald's case myself. But before I ever opened that dog up, I'd already seen more than enough. Because we didn't just find him — we worked on him. We worked on him hard. When we got to him, he was still alive. Barely. Dragging himself forward with just his front legs, the back half of his body limp and useless like it didn't belong to him anymore. And even then — even then — he was fighting to live. His breathing... I can still hear it. Every inhale whistled thin and sideways, like air was slipping out through a tear you couldn't see. He was dragging breath through pain that should've knocked him unconscious, but he fought with us, refused to quit. But bodies break in ways spirit can't fix. He held on long enough to look us in the eyes — long enough for us to tell him he wasn't alone anymore. And then he went quiet. Just... quiet. So when I performed the necropsy later, I already knew what I was going to find. His spine was shattered through the mid-thoracic vertebrae

— the place where control ends and helplessness begins. The vertebrae weren't cracked; they were crushed flat. Pancaked. The spinal cord underneath…HEY! I will kick you again. Do you understand? Pay attention. His right lung was bruised so violently you could see the shape of the impact in the tissue. And when I found pockets of air trapped where they didn't belong, I knew exactly why his breathing had sounded the way it did. The inside matched the sound. His diaphragm had a tear — small, but vicious — letting things grind and slip where nothing should ever touch. The liver showed blunt trauma…That dog's body told the whole story not of the injury itself, but of the kind of man who caused it. You know. Assholes like you who think discipline and cruelty are the same thing. You probably call it "teaching them right." Gerald was one of you. Born with a temper instead of a backbone. Oh. I see it in your eyes. You'd strangle the life out of me if you could. Fortunately for me, that will never happen. For one thing, I'm smarter than you are – and I'm backed by a whole team of brilliant people. We knew this wasn't Gerald's first time hurting an animal. Hell, half the folks in that trailer park could list the things they'd seen him do: kicking a cat off his porch, throwing a beer can at a stray, dragging his own dog by the collar until the poor thing choked. The kind of man who'd brag about being "old-school" when really, he was just mean. And it wasn't his first time in the system either. Gerald lived in a revolving door — in and out, in and out, anger management classes stapled onto probation, probation stapled onto fines he never paid. He was a regular face in the county clerk's office, a known headache for deputies, the type of man who always had a file that didn't have time to gather dust because he was always doing something petty and hateful that crossed lines. And that—right there—is about where our folks started paying attention. See, we never just spring out of nowhere. We study you. Our folks had been talking for months. Like-minded individuals, Seth calls us. Most folks think of us as extended family. People who don't share blood but share something deeper — conviction that sometimes you must take justice in your own hands as a community. We have the conviction to make a comprehensive strategic action plan and make it happen. We examine everything from the history of each case to determine if the abuse or neglect was intentional and a pattern. I can't convey how careful we are in trying to do the right thing. When we see a pattern of cruelty without remorse, we know it's time to act. You've met our extraction team. We didn't pick that name because it sounded tough. God knows we're not playing soldier. We picked it because it was honest. We extract the problems the system refuses to address. We pull out the rot before it spreads.

Seth and I helped shape the first team—six people who'd proven, time and again, that they could stay calm when others panicked, think clearly when others froze, and do what needed doing when everyone else turned away. When Gerald's case came across our table — broken dog, broken laws, broken system — every person in that room agreed without hesitation. But I'm not gonna bore you with the logistics of a complicated extraction. That's not what you're here for, and that sure as hell ain't what interests me. We're here to talk about comeuppance, motherfucker.

Chapter 5

Roll your eyes all you want at the justce coming your way – maybe don't let Miss Kay see you. She hates that and has a thing for eyes. Pretty blue things like that – she could do all kinds of things to…

I already told you that Gerald didn't go quickly. Must've been fueled by hate. He lasted ninety-something days with a spine that would never carry him again and a lung that refused to open all the way. Oh yeah. People can survive with a collapsed lung – it's not acutely fatal. If it's collapsed…right. It can be done to make every living minute feel like drowning. It's excruciatingly painful. A collapsed lung that doesn't kill you fast, makes every breath feel useless. Feels like a knife under the ribs that never comes out — sharp at the start, then burning, searing agony with every breath. And it's exhausting. Oh, of course we made sure to mirror all of Gerald's dog's injuries. He didn't respect her enough to name her, but we collectively named her Sophia in hopes she would survive. Sophia's injuries were fatal. We made sure Gerald's were too – eventually. None of us wanted to let him off easily again. So, while, yes – we did also hit him with his own sledgehammer, we stopped short of serious injury because we understood the bigger picture. I'm sure the blow to Gerald's spine was painful, but that wasn't what caused the damage. We did that. Severed his spinal cord in the same place and put the perfect hole in the back of his right lung and ensured he would remain relatively stable long enough to feel what he made Sophia endure. He couldn't walk. He couldn't stand. Gerald lived inside that half-life a long time. He had no remorse and spit vitriol and threats until it occurred to me that I could've silenced him at the start, so we strapped him down and I severed his vocal cords right then and there. Gerald wasn't some tragic patient lying there with dignity and quiet acceptance. When he pissed and shit himself, he wanted and would have killed every person on this compound. Paralysis steals more than movement. It steals control. And men like him? They never handled losing control well. At that point and even in his condition, he became a danger to us, and I wasn't going to have that. We reevaluated all our safety protocols. Each confinement and associated conditions are carefully planned out. I hadn't anticipated needing to cage him, but his behavior necessitated the upgrade. That's when we learned it's easiest to just high-pressure hose you off. It may have the benefit of debridement, but it mainly just stings like hell and carries who-knows-what types of pathogens into open wounds. If you're one of the lucky ones, you'll have a nice family of maggots to set up in that rough looking area-there—uh…that was a mandible…anyway-they could clean it for you. It looked nasty. With the heat and the rot and the way infection chews through a man who can't move. Gerald's wound over his ribs turned wet and sweet-smelling. Flies came first. Maggots followed. Not inside the lung — nothing could survive in there — but in the dead flesh around it, the part that had gone soft and gray. They fed on what the infection killed. You'd think the smell would be the worst! No! When he tried deep breaths and coughed, maggots flopping from the sticky hole sounded like someone trying to spit watermelon seeds for the first time. It was a horrible way to die. The system never gave him consequences. The folks out here did. And he felt every hour of it – well, half of it anyway. In the end, it wasn't the lung or the spine that killed him. Those just trapped him. What finished Gerald was infection — slow, creeping, hungry. His wounds went foul, his fever climbed, and his blood turned against him one organ at a time. Sepsis, they'd call it in a hospital. Out here, we just call it consequences. You have the day you deserve and we'll see you when we see you.

Chapter 6

Day 2

Afternoon. Well good for you! I'll get that 'two' on the board right now. Ok. Now. I think I'll tell you about Marissa today. Her story is short and you smell like your bowels have got to be empty because -DAMN! You know shit's bad when it makes me gag. I swear I'm going to need a shower and change of clothes -I might burn my clothes. Oh. Burning. Do you wonder how we dispose of bodies? I'm going to tell you anyway because, depending on you, we may have some time together and as an idealist – an optimist – I'd like to believe that end those last breaths you truly do understand and do feel remorse…and if you don't – the other side can deal with you.

Maybe this evening we can get you in a larger cage – did I say that? Now why would I ever give you a smidgen of hope. I'm sure Buddy hoped you would help him – shit! I'm sure Buddy hoped you would fucking feed him! Yeah, I heard your stomach growl. Starts to hurt, doesn't it? Like you could eat yourself from within. You can't think of anything else but food? Some mornings I just need more than coffee. Did you smell mine when I came in? Smells good doesn't it? We noted the coffee maker in that dumpster fire you called home. Your caffeine withdrawal headache is a bonus. Yeah, I had my first cup this morning with breakfast. You know some men can be so thoughtful. Seth said he got up early, so he made the morning team a huge spread this morning. He went big! Of course I have a world class professional kitchen, nutritionists, and a chef but Dan and Seth have been tight for a long time and (don't tell Dan) I think Seth is just as good. So, we had Belgian waffles – so light and fluffy-mmm-drenched in butter and syrup and bacon and sausage and fresh fruit…the eggs…oh those eggs are just like heaven…anyway…here's your meal for today. Water? Your eyes are probably starting to plead for? Mmmm wouldn't ice chips be wonderful? Remember – you're the monster here. Monsters don't get delightful ice chips. You can try to lick at the water when I hose you down in a bit. From Buddy's level of dehydration and the dry bowl at the time of extraction, my guess is his only saving grace was all the recent rain – yeah, I see it in your eyes. Hose confirmed. Don't worry though, I can drag you out in the rain if you prefer but your wounds are still fresh, we wouldn't want to leave you out to be nibbled on by some poor unfortunate creature. Scary, isn't it? When your own cruelty is reflected back? May you find redemption in the next life.

I'm going to need to turn you so I can spray the back and get all this shit gone. You may deserve the smell, but I do not. Oh, you can't turn? No shit Captain Obvious. You're nicely folded in your cute little cage with your little smushed up face and you're on top of turntable of sorts. We've thought of everything. Ew. This side smells worse.

Dadgum it! I'm running late today – reviewing a new case for possible extraction. But don't you worry. We let each and every one of you die by your own method. I will say that it is my opinion that you will be the new record keeper. Your age, general health, and excess weight give you a decent chance of surviving for weeks, months – shit if you don't die of infection, it might take you a year to starve. I actually don't know. I need to talk to the nutritionist. But I can assure you every aspect of Buddy's abuse and neglect we're considered, and we extrapolate as precisely as possible, so the offender's suffering mirrors that of the abused. All that adipose – fat – that you're packing that could drag this out – that's on you. I'm actually rooting for you to hang in there for a bit. I don't want all that lard to fuck up my crematorium. I told you – when you have the money and time to think of everything…

Even Marissa – see? You thought I'd forgotten. Marissa Barnell. Most vapid bitch you'd ever meet. Yeah – you saw on the news…still missing…police having difficulty tracking her last whereabouts because she liked to go out…social butterfly…but they never found her or her car. Just one last cell ping over by the drive-thru daiquiri place. Not just a cold case…a dead-end case. We're proud of her case because she was our first car recycling. Up until then our extractions were like alien abductions. One minute an asshole is at home and the next they aren't. You know. Professionals, am I right? Things are a little different for vehicles. We've got a handful of folks out here who can take apart anything with an engine. Welders, mechanics, and those born-with-a-wrench types. Give them a day and a cutting torch and they'll turn a pickup into dog furniture, kennel wire, and a water trough. Whatever's left gets hauled off with the other junkers for shredding. Just rural recycling done by people who know metal better than they know their own birthdays. Part of your cage is from her BMW. That white BMW 3-Series, the kind of car people finance because they want to look expensive from a distance and the kind of drivers who usually menace others because they think it's their road. Marissa had it all. The rhinestone plate frame, pink steering wheel cover, dog's name—Bella—written in metallic gold cursive on the back glass like a designer label. Bella wasn't a pet. She was something for more attention getting selfies. She was a breathing charm bracelet. Bella was an accessory. When someone is so selfish that they only care about themselves, they don't even consider others. The necropsy showed everything. The chronic vape exposure. How sick Bella was becoming. Feeding shitty human food to a dog for views and likes is not cute, it hurts them. Bella had fatty liver changes, inflamed pancreas, the kind of GI scarring you only see when someone feeds a dog shit their body isn't built to handle. But that's not what killed her. Neglect did that. Being left in the car in Texas weather did that. Some people feel torn at the 'left them in the car' cases. Not this one. Marissa had made an appointment at a new nail salon as her prior manicurist could not satisfy her — none of them ever could. So anyway, this new manicurist couldn't be swayed to allow Bella to stay for Marissa's appointment. Determined not to be inconvenienced and having her nails perfect to her specifications without delay, Marissa told the shop owner she could call and have her boyfriend get Bella. She then took Bella to car. Tiny Bella was tossed into the backseat like trash. The shop owner had somehow not seen a thing as she was with another customer and earnestly thought the boyfriend had the dog. She was told Marissa's boyfriend lived just behind the strip mall and was just a short drive away. What kind of vapid monster leaves her dog in the car for three hours so she can get XL coffin nails, chrome, encapsulated glitter, bling clusters, and whatever 'snatched cuticles' are supposed to be? All that detail for something she'd chip opening her purse. Marissa wasn't absent-minded when she left Bella to die and she wasn't stupid enough to think the interior of a car in July in Texas heat is a safe place to hang out. You know that's what's so mind boggling – she had to have known she was giving that dog a death sentence. Maybe the dog's views were down on her social media, and she wanted a change of accessories. Oh, and she also tried to blame the manicurist for "taking too long". Dogs don't just 'get hot' in a car. They panic. They suffocate in heat too thick for panting to fix. Their heart races, their brain burns, their organs begin to shut down one by one. They vomit, they collapse, they cry. They're scared the whole time — confused, trapped, desperate for air that won't save them. It's not quick. It's not quiet. And it's not painless. Bella was terrified and alone and died a horrible death and her death was a choice. We all grieved Bella. In the common room there's a beautiful art piece of the Tree of Life. Each precious soul we've lost to an abuser has their ashes turned into a glass leaf, glowing in the branches. A whole canopy of color and memory. We walk past it every day. We touch the leaves. Not out of ritual, but out of reminder. Every one of those leaves is a name that should've had more time. Every one of them is a reason we do what we do. Bella's leaf is soft blue with a gold shimmer in the curl of the glass. Seth picked that color. She was forced into Pepto-pink her whole life and he thought she'd appreciate a peaceful blue. It hangs on the east side of the tree, where the morning sun hits it first.

But I don't want us to part with you thinking sweet, peaceful thoughts. You don't deserve that. Marissa's fate matched Bella's. After extraction, in which we kept her sedated, any means for her to truly fight back were removed – her keys, her phone - which we'd left in the restaurant parking lot...we even disabled her car engine and horn...then we welded her doors shut and reinforced all windows with plexiglass. Adults hold on longer, sure. They sweat more, fight more, stay conscious longer. But heat doesn't care. By the time a full day passes in a sealed car, the panic alone has done half the work, and the strain on the heart and brain does the rest. No one walks away from that unchanged. If it's hot outside. Our issue with Marissa is we didn't get clear opportunity for extraction until the weather wasn't right for her punishment. It was too mild, too forgiving — so our folks got creative in that way only rural people with too much scrap metal know how. They set her car chassis over the old fire pit we use for cookouts, just rolled it right over the hole. Now we have replicated conditions as close as possible, but like I said, you chose when you're gonna give it up. We set up the fire to burn low and slow. We lit the match the moment she came out of sedation. Marissa woke up exactly the way you'd expected she would — loud, offended, and absolutely convinced the universe had made a mistake. She didn't even clock her situation at first! She reached for the rearview mirror to check her face and hair. That's always the first thing women like her do: not assess danger, not figure out where they are, but make sure the glam stays intact. Priorities. Always the same. She wasn't thinking about Bella yet. She wasn't thinking about anything real. She was thinking about herself, and only herself, because that's the only language Marissa knows how to speak. She woke up like she was having a customer service crisis and needed a manager post haste. We watched her slapped the window with the flat of her hand — careful not to chip her new chrome nails — even as she continued to threaten us should one of her precious tips get damaged. She was vapid until the end. Once she realized she didn't know where she was, her car wouldn't start, and her purse was missing, the entitled rage really came out. She behaved like she believed she'd been caught up in some 'Taken' scenario where she was snatched for her prized beauty. Like she was some treasure someone would search for. We knew what she really was- trash. She was perpetually the messy drunk who's hot enough for some opportunistic asshole to fuck. She's also so obnoxious they want her gone in the morning. Nobody was looking for her. Only Marissa cared about Marissa. She hollered out offers of all sorts of sexual favors in return for her release. She threatened. She begged. She was as hateful as a harpy and manipulative as succubus until the end. Died being as shitty of a human as she was in life. Like I said, she initially didn't panic but boy when she did – it was quite a show. At first, she was gulping at the air like it should've been cooler, fresher, or something. Looked like a guppy with those big ass duck lips. You know that air got thicker by the minute. You've been in a hot car before — you know that feeling when the air gets stale and heavy? Multiply it. When the smoke started seeping in through the vents we'd mostly sealed, it wasn't a cloud, just enough to sting. She rubbed her eyes like a toddler and only made it worse. I imagine that by then she couldn't see straight, couldn't tell what was smoke and what was tears. At this point we still had pretty good visibility, soot hadn't accumulated yet. Was still screaming, but the coughing kept cutting her off. I'm betting that the heat and the grit in the air had her throat raw within minutes. She kept grabbing the handle, slapping the window, yelling every threat she could think of. Still trying to act in charge even while choking on her own breath. And it just kept getting hotter. She didn't go quietly. Didn't go gracefully. She went exactly the way she lived: loud, selfish, and miserable. We threw her ashes in the cesspool beneath you. She's mixing with your shit now.

You have the night you deserve.

Chapter 7

Day 3

I see you're up already and ready for that three. Hard to sleep when you can't lay down, huh? You probably should've thought of that. Hmmm. Your swelling has gone down a bit. No maggots yet. Ok then. Let's get you hosed off and tell you another story. You get a twofer today. Ashlee and Cody Hunt. You're going to want to imagine stereotypical meth heads. Wild-eyed, rotted teeth, twitchy jaws, and each with an explosive temper - always ready to go off. We know that they went off on BB. He was covered in scars and wounds that looked exactly like cigarette burns in various stages of healing. We renamed the dog BB. They named him Big Ballz. With a Z. Because of course they did. I'm sure they stood stand on their porch, cigarette hanging off their lip, hollering, 'BALLZ! Get over here!' like it was high comedy. BB is a pit mix – not that we could in his emaciated state. They'd shackled him to a pole with chain and prong collar when he was maybe six months old, back when he still had a puppy face and big dumb paws. And then they left him. And as he grew — because dogs do that — the collar didn't. It just dug in. Slowly. Every day. Every week. By the time one of the neighbors got brave enough to call for help, the prongs weren't on his skin — they were in it. The neck had swollen around the metal like the body had tried to swallow the pain. His fur was matted. The wound smelled like something that had been hurting for a long time. And you know what that dog did when someone finally approached him? He wagged his tail. Soft. Slow. Small little thump-thump like he thought he was the one in trouble for something. Dogs are always loyal to people who don't deserve them. People like those assholes. When we got the report, it wasn't even a debate. Embedded collar case. Chronic neglect. Predictable pattern. You don't have to be a detective to spot the type. So, we scheduled an immediate extraction. Not that you deserve a happy fact, but BB survives to this day and found a loving home with one of us. We had a decision with the couple. Would they learn better if apart or together? In the end, we decided to do both. See that bigger room to your right? We put them in there together, one in each corner. The boys rigged up a little winch system that pulled them toward each other whenever they acted up. Any resistance cinched their custom prong collars tighter. They were such vile, stupid creatures they kept triggering it themselves. Could've dragged it out for months if they'd had a shred of sense, but no—they managed to asphyxiate themselves in under a day. Their extraction and disposal took longer.

Hmm. Well since I'm not done with you today, why don't I tell you a bit more about my background? You already know a bit about my childhood trauma, the money I won, our gorgeous facilities… might as well give you the origin story of Sweet Caroline's. So back when I was little, the singer Neil Diamond was everywhere. My mom, my Aunt Brenda, and Aunt Brenda's oldest boy, Nathan — they wore that man's records out. 'Sweet Caroline' on repeat like it was the national anthem. Aunt Brenda even named their dog Caroline because of it. Big floppy-eared mutt who'd howl along like she thought she was on key. Then I came along. And because my family is exactly the brand of chaotic you'd expect, they let Nathan — who was maybe eight at the time — pick my name. He adored that dog. And you see where this is going. My mom and my aunt will swear up and down I was named after the song. Nathan will swear up and down I was named after the dog. He used to chase me around singing, 'Sweeet Caroline — woof, woof, woof!' Real comedian, that one. Anyway, Nathan and I grew up thick as thieves. Both of us went to vet school. Seth joined the mix and the three of us daydreamed about a place like this long before we had any means to make it real. So, when I opened my first tiny grooming shop — barely more than a glorified shed with a tub — we named it Sweet Caroline's. Part joke. Part family tribute. And that's how the whole thing started.

If I see you tomorrow maybe I'll tell you about Jeremy Swanson and the god-awful shit he did to his grandmother's cat, Pearl. Let's just say it's an explosive story. Oh, and you might want to make that big of food last. I don't think anyone is going to a store today and we might be out. Have the afternoon you deserve.

Chapter 8

Day 4

Day Four, and look at that — you finally got company. I told you they were coming. Told you the air here runs thick and warm enough to draw anything with wings. And sure enough, they've found you. Right there along the ear. Feel that? That's not your own skin crawling around. Don't flinch — I'm not touching them. Blowflies love decomposition — and dirty, untreated wounds that smell like that. They love dead or dying tissue fast, because their larvae survive best there. Busy little things. Funny thing is, you'd think that smell would bother me by now, but it doesn't. It's the sound I notice. You hear that? That faint little fizzing noise? Like a carbonated drink settling? That's them. Blowfly larvae always sound like that when they've settled in — like a soda dying out or rain falling on paper. Now, here's the thing. We don't know what their end effect on you is going to be. Uncontrolled larvae are unpredictable. Sometimes they stick to the necrotic tissue — the dead bits your body gave up on — and they chew away just enough to keep a person hanging on a little longer. Strange sort of mercy, if you want to call it that. Other times? They introduce whatever bacteria they've picked up along the way. Then everything gets angrier — redder, wetter, hotter. Inflammation spreads. The whole area turns into this putrid, swollen mess that throbs with its own heartbeat. That's what happens when there's no control, no cleaning, no sterile anything. Things just… spiral. The pain stays. The burning stays. The itching gets worse. And the psychological part—oh, that's the real killer. It's not knowing. The feeling of them moving even when they're still. The way your brain tries to convince itself the whole side of your head is crawling, and you feel like they'll eat their way right into your fucking brain. It breaks most people. We'll see how you do. Maggots didn't kill Buddy because we saved him. You won't be so lucky.

Let's talk about infection. Earl Thimons. That motherfucker. Scarlett was a Great Dane because she was injured so severely as a puppy, her left ankle bore a heinous scar with the skin scarcely able to cover the gap as she grew. He swore the leg was a parent stepping on the puppy. That became harder to believe after her subsequent treatment. He left her chained in the fiercest, most dangerous arctic weather that Texas has had in years. Great Danes are intolerant of cold. Her ears froze to her head and her paws to the ground! It must've been excruciating and she was chained out in the open through a storm so dangerous people and livestock died! If his neighbor wouldn't have been sent home from work early and called the sheriff, she would've been dead by nightfall on the first night. If it would've been later in the day – I don't know if we would've been able to get to her. She still had to fight for her life and frostbite doesn't just thaw out and call it a day — it keeps hurting long after the cold lets go. The tissues that froze on her — the tips of her ears, the end of her tail, that one tiny toe — they didn't come back. They'd gone gray and leathery, then turned this awful, angry red around the edges as her body tried to wall it off. We did what you always do in cases like that: kept her warm, kept her hydrated, kept infection from taking her the rest of the way. The dead parts had to go, eventually. They weren't doing her any favors, just holding rot and pain. So, she lost the tip of one ear, a sliver of her tail, and that one little toe that never woke back up. The healing was slow, too. Frostbite wounds don't follow the rules. They blister, they weep, they flare up with every change in weather. And when the tissue around it is trying to survive, it burns like fire — a deep, throbbing ache that never seems to shut up. Poor baby needed extra calories and protein just to knit the edges closed. Her body was working overtime, and you could see it in her eyes — exhausted, hurting, but stubborn enough to keep going. And she did. Because dogs do. They fight harder than most people ever have. She fought harder than that mean old bastard. And you know dogs — they don't cling to cruelty the way people do. They remember the shape of a bad man, the scent of danger, but they don't sit around replaying it. Sunny only shows it when she sleeps. Every now and then she'll whimper in her dreams, soft and scared, like some echo of what she went through is still trying to climb out. That's the only time my heart aches for her past. The rest of the time, she's too busy living. She has such a joyous soul. She's usually leaning on me – if I'm not here. You don't get to meet her.

Earl was a tricky one. Like you, he lived way in the boonies. Y'all like those long ass, dead-end country roads, with the long ass driveways don't y'all? Earl liked his guns too and we had record of him threatening to "pepper that ass" when complaining to his neighbor about a loose dog. That dog went missing. Earl was suspected but nothing came of it. Two years later, a few drunk and disorderly charges, a few assault and battery charges, and we get a call from the darndest of places-Amazon. Earl let Amazon up that drive to deliver, and the weather hadn't deteriorated the roads to be completely impassable. The driver immediately took photos and called the emergency in to the sheriff. Don is a good man. We've never had a better sheriff. I got the call within minutes of Don. Turns out the Amazon driver, Anthony was dating Don's middle daughter! He just called up his future father-in-law. Talk about fate! I wouldn't have believed it even if I saw it in a book! We were meant to take out that hermit motherfucker Earl and I was meant to give Sunny the life she deserves! Don made it to Earl's within thirty minutes, and I was there in forty-three minutes. Don already had Earl hogtied on the ground and Sunny draped in a blanket-realizing the gravity of her situation not knowing how to help. I'll never forget the look of relief in Sunny's eyes as I finally held her. I don't think I've ever hugged Don so tight. I still owe him that hot chocolate. Don understands the pattern — the same types of cases that always get the perpetual wrist slaps. The ones that drag on, get pled down, get dismissed, and leave the animals to keep suffering because nobody with authority ever seems to take it seriously. He does. No paperwork. No trace. Earl lived so far off-grid nobody would've missed him. No kin, no visitors, no one driving up that dirt track unless they were lost. Man could've keeled over in his own kitchen and the vultures would've found him before the county did. Nobody but Amazon ever went out there. No orders. No deliveries. Earl's long gone and his Amazon package – that's still on his porch. We didn't have to do nothing fancy for Earl to get what he had coming. We just brought him here and left him outside like the trash. We intervened just enough for most of him to survive the cold. Then we watched as he rots. The suffering he caused and the suffering he endured balanced the scales of justice but after seeing it – smelling it – I can tell you cold and heat are two of the most brutal ways a creature can suffer. And here's the thing that still makes my blood boil: it took hundreds of dogs freezing to death during that storm before Texas finally pulled its head out of its ass and passed a law to stop people from chaining animals out in the open. Too damn late for all the ones that died shaking and alone in the ice. Too damn late for every dog that screamed into the wind while their owners stayed warm inside. Earl didn't just pay for what he did to her — he was a little sliver of justice for all the dogs that never got any. We made sure the cold didn't kill outright, the rot did. Frostbite looks quiet at first — numb, stiff, pale — but that's just the body giving up on the parts it can't save. After a day or two, the dead areas turn dark and hard, like burnt wood. That's necrosis. Once that happens, the body has two choices: seal the dead tissue off, or let infection slip in around the edges. And Earl? He didn't have the strength, the warmth, or the blood flow to fight anything. The necrosis cracked open, let bacteria flood in, and the whole area went hot and swollen while the center stayed cold and dead. That's when the infection spread. First local, then deeper. His immune system panicked, then faltered. His blood pressure crashed. His organs started tapping out one by one. In the end, it wasn't the cold that finished him — it was the body-wide collapse that followed. I hope it was absolutely excruciating. Based on the agony etched on his face, it was.

Chapter 9

Day 6

Well long time no see. I won't apologize for yesterday because I'm certain you forced Buddy to have days without food because you were too drunk to care or remember. We had an extraordinary case. Someone I've been waiting to see since I first met him as a child. Max Richardson. I was rooting for Max. I really was. I first met him when his mother moved into our apartment complex. I don't remember her name because she never seemed to be around and wasn't fully present when she was. The property manager released her from her lease because there was an incident with Max and a neighborhood cat. You can't tell me that little boy hadn't witnessed either something horrible or survived something horrible to cause him to violently violate a cat with a pencil. I've shuddered in revulsion at the thought plenty of times over the years, but it was easier to process because I'd convinced myself to be certain of only my select scenarios — after being thrown out of the apartment complex, the mom immediately got counseling for the kid and everything was ok or more likely, the kid quickly escalated his psychotic behavior and has long been locked up in one detention center or another. I didn't know how right I'd been but repeat offender didn't begin to describe the depravity of that kid. Max, now in his late twenties – had been sent to counseling his mother back then, or so the apartment manager was told. In truth, the moment a child hurts an animal like that, a whole line of people gets involved: school counselors, social workers, the county behavioral health folks, whatever overstretched system is still functioning. And they all try — they always try — because five-year-olds aren't supposed to understand violence, much less choose it. But Max never responded to any of it. He went through every program they could shove him into crisis therapy, mandated evaluations, short-term stabilization units. They kept handing him off like a live grenade no one wanted to drop, and every time they thought he'd leveled out, he'd prove them wrong. The reports followed him from county to county — defiance, escalation, lack of empathy, a pattern they write in careful language, but everyone knows the meaning of. By the time he was a teenager, the file on him could've filled a drawer. Fights. Threats. Animal control calls. Assaults in school. Every expert who tried to intervene eventually wrote the same thing, just dressed up in clinical phrasing: Max understood right and wrong perfectly well. He just didn't care. That kid was a fucking psychopath. When they're cute and little everybody wants to save them. Nobody wants to admit a child might be rotten to the core. And once Max hit adulthood, the safety nets stopped catching him. That's how he ended up back on our radar. That's why I'd been waiting to see him again. And the sheriff's call that finally brought his name back into my life? Don told me a neighbor had seen Max grab a cat and shove a lit firecracker right up its ass before letting it go. They couldn't even charge him for what he'd done to the animal — only for setting off fireworks during a burn ban. Max knew the loopholes. He'd always known. We searched. We found droplets of blood, little arcs in the dirt… but we never found that cat. And I don't care how tough an old tom might be — nothing survives that kind of trauma. You don't need anatomy to understand what an explosion does to soft, delicate places. Pain like that is unimaginable. A creature would either die fast or die terrified. I'm sure Max walked away from it like he'd flicked a cigarette butt. It probably wouldn't surprise you if I told you we have a brilliant psychologist on our team. And not the 'read your aura and align your chakras' kind. We're talking old-school Bureau pedigree — someone who spent twenty years profiling violent offenders for the FBI. She's the one who keeps us grounded in the truth of what we're dealing with. She builds the psychological profiles, helps us understand exactly what kind of creature we've got in front of us, and designs the comeuppance therapies so the punishment actually fits the pathology. And she's not just here for them. She's here for us. Every one of our folks carries trauma — years of seeing animals mangled, burned, starved, drowned, frozen, beaten, or abandoned. You don't witness that kind of cruelty over and over without it carving something out of you. So, she keeps our heads straight enough to keep doing the work. When she looked at Max's history, his escalation, the way he hurt small animals without hesitation or remorse, she didn't mince words. She said his pattern fits the extreme end of antisocial pathology — the kind where empathy never develops and never will. The kind where fear doesn't register, consequences don't matter, and pain is just another sensation that never slows them down. Her exact line was, 'There isn't a creature on this earth that's safe around someone like him. Not an animal, not a person, not a neighbor, not a stranger.' According to her, Max doesn't attach, doesn't bond, doesn't recognize suffering as real unless it's happening to him. And even then, he doesn't learn from it. He just moves on to the next thing he can break. With the realization that no amount of suffering would bring him to understanding, everyone decided the most prudent course would be to focus on his last offense. Don't think we didn't consider giving him

the big pencil first though. He deserved to suffer!
Let me shove even a small explosive up your ass
and you will never be the same!

I've stuffed a few piñatas in my time but not like
this. While Max deserved to be awake and aware,
he presented an unprecedented danger to my
team according to our assessments. He was
massive, mean, fit, and very strong. Not that any
of that gave us a pause. We work with wild
animals often. We just needed to use a bit of
honey to seduce and drug the bear. We haven't
found a walking red flag that the twins couldn't
take down. Lindsey and Landon. Two of the most
gorgeous humans to ever walk the earth and part
of my family. My niece and nephew. In their last
year of veterinary school. We all understand each
assignment. Narrowing Max down wasn't hard
once we had access to his file. A man like him
leaves fingerprints everywhere he goes — not
literal ones, but patterns. Same counties. Same
payday weekends. Same cheap gas stations on
the route between them. Same way he'd burn
through a new phone number every few months
but always kept the same cheap model. Our
psychologist mapped it out like she was tracing
migration routes. Predators orbit comfort. They
circle familiar terrain even when they think they're
unpredictable. He never hit the same bar twice —
that part was true — but he stayed inside the

same triangle of dive bars, truck stops, and late-night liquor stores. He had a rhythm, even if he didn't know it. That's how she spotted him. One glance across that sticky, neon-lit dive and she knew. He matched the photo down to the posture — the slouched shoulders, the scanning eyes, the fake easy smile he put on for women who didn't know better. Lindsey was there within an hour. Gave him time to get a few in him already and came in smoking hot. She walked right past him once, slow enough for him to catch a whiff of perfume and fantasy, and that was it. The trap sprung itself. I'll let you fill in the details of when she slipped something into his drink — you know the moment. Max never saw it coming. Predators never prepare for a bigger predator. What the bar saw was simple: A gorgeous, drop-dead woman — legs for days, skirt barely legal, hair cascading, the kind of body men elbow each other over — hauling some sloppy, stumbling drunk toward the door. He looked pathetic, half-folded over himself, muttering nonsense. She looked annoyed, doing that tight-lipped smile women do when they're 'so, so sorry, he's had too much.' Nobody questioned it. Bars see that scene every weekend. But a beautiful woman dragging a dumb, helpless man out the door is practically folklore though and people would remember here. Unfortunately, nobody remembered him. They remembered an angel rescuing her friend. We'd decided to be generous with dosage because we were worried about safety. He stayed out until we fi led his ass with 20 black cat firecrackers pushed into a balloon with the balloon neck and fuse dangling out like a little green tail screaming "GO". We put a stitch in just to be sure it stayed and then we left him our newly installed blast cell while we went for a delightful brunch. We figured since we were doing fireworks that evening, we should celebrate, so the folks set the table that morning and we all came together. Usually, breakfast starts early and, on the go, because we've got to care for the animals, but when you've built a community, there's always a helping hand to make things work. By the time Max finally started to stir, our folks were finishing breakfast. We did it right — big spread, everything fresh. Lemon-ricotta pancakes stacked high, rosemary hash browns crisped to perfection, fresh-baked sourdough, and a platter of roasted vegetables that smelled like heaven. No bacon, no sausage, no greasy shit. I bet you'd kill for some bacon about now? Can you remember the smell of bacon? You'll never smell it again.

Smell! Now that smell was the worst! Burned ass. Burned hair. Burned shit. The sulfur from the firecracker…I gag just thinking about it. From the initial howl at waking up with a newly stuffed ass, I'm guessing it wasn't comfortable. He went from pleading to threatening – you literally all do once the pain hits. And what is it about you assholes having main character syndrome and thinking you're so desirable that you've been captured to fulfill someone's lurid sex den. I mean if you woke up shackled to the four corners and spread eagle, you might draw some conclusions too. We didn't correct him when he thought he'd been raped. We counted those hours of his pain and despair as justice for the women he likely violated. In the evening, we gathered and lit the fuse which we'd extended for safety. I don't think he realized what was happening until the pain hit. That – made me wish I'd severed his vocal cords. I had to put my earbuds in! He didn't last long though. That kind of extreme pain kicks the body into overdrive, and then everything crashes. You could see it in his eyes first — that wild, frantic shine people get when the pain stops being something they can grit through and they completely unravel. Screaming and begging for it to end. So, his body shut down and ended it for him.

Wait. Silly me! You probably heard all the racket yesterday! That was Max.

Maybe I'll see you tomorrow, maybe I won't. Have the night you deserve.

Chapter 10

Day 7

Hey! Look who's made it a whole week! And the new diet suits you! Not that we're going to weigh you, but I do believe some of that chunk is coming off! If this keeps up, we're going to need to tighten that cage a bit. Just kidding! I don't think you'll live that long. You did live long enough to lose your buddies. Uncontrolled larvae never stick around for more than a handful of days — they feed, they bloat up, and then they wriggle off to finish their life cycle somewhere else. They come in fast and leave fast, but the infection and inflammation they kick up can linger... Where the bridge of your nose was crushed - that's not looking good. Oh Well. C'est La Vie. Let's get you sprayed off, shall we?

One thing all abusers like you have in common, most of you are men and all of you treat animals like they're disposable. Sadly, throwing animals from moving vehicles is a documented and depressingly common cruelty pattern. Cruel and stupid because there are still good people that bring in injured animals and call it in. We folks have broad access to traffic cameras. They aren't getting away from us. By now you may be thinking, "but Caroline, how can you make that many people disappear?" Because nobody looks for assholes like you and I have the system on my side. I have good folks – everywhere. I love it when I look in your eyes and see I'm right. Feel that? That's the dull ache of hope leaving. Nobody's going to come looking for you because every choice you've ever made in life made sure nobody would ever want you. Mean-spirited. Yeah-you're getting exactly what you deserve, aren't you? Have you started to think about how Buddy felt? You need to feel to really understand.

Now pay attention. I'm tired, your smell is giving me a headache. Or the stress of trying to teach someone like you is giving me a headache. Ugh. Twice in my life I've witnessed a kitten tossed into traffic. The first time I was just a kid-before cell phones and ubiquitous cameras. The second time was about sixteen years ago; we were crossing the bridge over Lake Palestine and saw the driver toss a tiny orange and white ball of fluff out the window. By the time we realized what it was we were past. You know any poor baby tossed out a window at seventy miles per hour doesn't stand a chance of survival. We looped back around and sure enough the kitten hadn't survived. So, we named her Marmalade, she became an orange and gold leaf, and we found the motherfucker who treated her like trash. By now I hope you appreciate the creativity it takes for us folks to match your depravity. I find that creative people are the most loving people and often they're the most fun to be around. And -I'll tell you some of the simplest things are the best solutions. You may have heard yesterday's shrills and thrills but our helipad is on the other side of the property — you may not be aware that we also have our own helicopter. Cleochopptera. We think it's funny. So…yeah. That was the solution. We take 'em up about thirty-three feet and drop them. I'll admit dropping them while shackled feet and wrist isn't ideal, but we can't risk an incident. Chad was the first of many over the last thirteen years. Chad wasn't like Max. Max was calculated malice — slow, deliberate, fascinated with suffering. Chad was the other kind. The simpler kind. The kind of man who didn't think past five minutes and didn't care past five feet. Chad lived in a permanent state of low-grade anger — always inconvenienced, always put-upon, always one small irritation away from punching a wall. He wasn't plotting anything. He wasn't masking anything. He just didn't value life. Any life. That's how you end up with a man who throws a kitten out the window of an F-150 like trash. No remorse. No hesitation. No second thought. Just a flick of the wrist from someone so hollow inside he doesn't understand why anyone else would care. But people cared and he would understand that. Him being afraid of heights and having "a panic attack" at take-off – that was chef's kiss sweet. We didn't rush to him after the fall. It'd had been a long morning already and we all were in desperate need of coffee. We got to him about two hours later-I guess? He wasn't dead but he was fucked up for sure. A fall of roughly thirty-three feet often leaves a body looking like it tried to land in several directions at once. Just absolute internal chaos — bilateral lower-extremity fractures, lumbar or thoracic spine compression injuries, and pelvic breaks -that force shoots up through the legs like a shockwave… Even if their head doesn't hit directly, that stop can cause subdural bleeding, concussion…We've seen it all - pulmonary contusions, rib fractures, sometimes a partially collapsed lung from the ribs bowing inward…and the soft tissues…they go splat like overripe fruit. I don't remember the extent of Chad's injuries, but they were extensive and he died an agonizing death. Let's be real though – all deaths here are agonizing – yours will be no different.

Chapter 11

Day 8

Hey! You still with me? Oh. Damn. You're fading. I can see it. Don't fight it — there's nothing left here for you to hold on to anyway. And no, I don't hate you – none of us hate you. You are not worth that energy. What we feel is… resolution. Balance finding itself. You handed your pain down to the helpless, and the universe finally handed it back to you. That's symmetry. I'm not without pity. I think every creature deserves at least one moment of truth before the end, even someone like you. And look at you now — you finally understand. Maybe not with words, but I can see it in your eyes. The recognition. The reckoning. The acceptance. What waits for you after this isn't my business. That's between you and whatever keeps the books on the other side. Maybe you'll come back…softer. Kinder. A little less… you. If so, that's the only mercy you've earned. As for us? Our work goes on. It has to. Our folks believe in carrying good forward, in making sure the scales stay honest. Sustainability — that's the word we use. Sustaining the good work. Sustaining justice no one else wants to touch. We do that. I do that. You won't be the last to find your way here. The world is full of people like you. Everyone has to pay the consequences in life. You're just the one paying it today.

Acknowledgments

To my husband — thank you for putting up with all my creepy shit and supporting me no matter how wild my dreams are.